# Calico and Tin Horns

# CALICO AND TIN HORNS

*by Candace Christiansen / paintings by* THOMAS LOCKER

Dial Books New York

*For Agnes*

—C.C. and T.L.

Published by Dial Books
A Division of Penguin Books USA Inc.
375 Hudson Street
New York, New York 10014

Designed by Nancy R. Leo
Printed in the U.S.A.
First Edition
1 3 5 7 9 10 8 6 4 2

Library of Congress Cataloging in Publication Data

Christiansen, Candace.
Calico and tin horns / Candace Christiansen ; paintings by
Thomas Locker. — 1st ed.
p.   cm.
Summary: Hannah's parents think that she is too young to be involved
in their resistance against their unfair landlord, until the sheriff's posse
comes after her father and his fellow rebel farmers and
Hannah is able to sound the warning signal.
ISBN 0-8037-1179-4. — ISBN 0-8037-1180-8 (lib. bdg.)
[1. Landlord and tenant—Fiction. 2. Farm life—Fiction.
3. Self-reliance—Fiction.]
I. Locker, Thomas, 1937–  ill. II. Title.
PZ7.C45287Cal 1992   [E]—dc20   91-3706   CIP   AC r91

The art for each picture consists of an oil painting that is
color-separated and reproduced in full color.

*In the early years of the American nation,*
certain wealthy landowners lived like feudal lords in grand manor houses along the Hudson River Valley in New York State. After the American Revolution these landowners promised to sell some of their lands to the returning war veterans, on condition that the veterans-turned-farmers would clear the land and share their harvests with the landowners for seven years. For generation after generation the farmers worked the land, passing it along to their sons, and their sons' sons. Still, the landowners ignored their promises and refused to sell the land outright, but continued to demand their share of the farmers' crops and livestock.

In 1844 the farmers banded together in a group that called itself "the Calico Indians," so named because the farmers identified their cause with that of the Boston Tea Party patriots seventy-one years before, who had dressed in calico costumes as a way of disguising themselves. The farmers also wanted to be associated with the nobler themes of Native American culture, and in particular with the idea of free access to land.

To prevent being recognized and arrested, the farmers disguised themselves with sheepskin masks, with holes cut out for their eyes, noses, and mouths. These were often decorated with beards, horns, feathers, or a horse's tail. They had no thought of being mistaken for "Indians" themselves—there were, in fact, almost no Native Americans living in the area at that time.

In the corner of our farm, in a meadow of wildflowers, there is a place where I go when I'm upset. Around the meadow is a stone wall my grandfather built, and when I climb it I can see the Van Rensselaers' big manor house, several miles away. My father takes me to that house every year, when all the farmers in the valley have to give a share of their crops to Mr. Van Rensselaer. I used to love to go and see the ladies in their fine dresses, the neat, mowed lawns, and the big house with all its sparkling windows. But this year we didn't go.

The trouble began one morning when I came in from doing my chores, and saw my mother sewing on a piece of calico cloth. The cloth was blue, and blue is my favorite color. I hoped that it was something for me, but when I asked, Mother put her sewing away and answered crossly, "Never mind, Hannah, it has nothing to do with little girls."

The look on her face and her sharp answer hurt me. Now I really wanted to know what Mother was doing that was so secret. I went outside to look for my father. When I found him in the barn, he and my older brother were working together on some pieces of leather. They looked surprised when I came in and they quickly hid their work from me. Before I could ask any questions, my father told me to go back out and play. It seemed unfair—my brother knew what was going on—why wouldn't anyone tell me? My family always thought I was too little!

That night I lay awake, confused and angry. Suddenly I heard the sound of horses, and men's voices out in the yard. Running to my window, I saw a group of riders. They were wearing leather masks, and calico shirts and pants.

I heard one man say, "We'll pay no more harvest rent! If Van Rensselaer sends his sheriff, we'll drive him off our mountain." Then two men dressed in the same calico clothing came out of our barn and rode away with the others into the night.

For the next few weeks there was a lot more farm work for my mother and me to do. My father and my brother were often away at secret meetings. Once, I heard my father tell my brother that the sheriff had brought a posse to make one of our neighbors leave his farm. I was frightened, but still no one would tell me what it was all about.

Then one morning when we were weeding the garden, I heard the faint sound of a dinner horn. This was strange because it wasn't near dinnertime. Then I heard it again. The sound was coming down the mountain from a neighbor's farm. Father ran to the porch, seized our dinner horn, and blew it. Then he disappeared into the barn. A few moments later, leading our two horses, he and my brother came out. They were dressed in calico and were wearing leather masks, and they carried their rifles. They got on the horses and galloped away toward the river.

After they left, my mother was pale and silent. "Go up the hill and pick some berries, Hannah," she said, "and later we'll make a pie." I was worried, but I started up the hillside. Since the summer had been hot, I had to climb higher and higher to find some ripe berries. When I reached the very top of the hill, I began to fill my pail. Suddenly, in the distance I noticed a cloud of dust rising from the old Albany road. It was the sheriff, riding his horse, followed by a small army, and they were heading straight toward our farm.

All at once I knew that our farm was in danger! But my father had gone down to the river — I had to warn him! I ran down a steep shortcut, tripping over stones and roots, and gooseberry thorns tore my dress. I started to shout when I got close to home, but no one answered.

No one was home. Mother must have gone over to our neighbor's farm. But the sheriff and his army were coming closer every minute. I knew what I had to do then. I grabbed the dinner horn from its hook on the porch, ran out to the barn, and scrambled up to the hayloft. I blew the horn with all my might.

I listened but nothing happened. The valley was silent. I blew the horn again, and in the distance I finally heard a horn answering, then another, and another. Horns rang out from up and down the whole mountain.

In just a few minutes masked riders galloped past our house from both directions. I thought I recognized my father riding with the others. They were all headed right for the sheriff's small army.

I could see the riders and the sheriff and his men as they caught sight of each other. The riders shouted war whoops and fired their rifles into the air. The sheriff's men stopped, and seeing that they were outnumbered, turned and ran.

The sheriff himself was thrown from his horse and was captured. The masked men tied him to his saddle and led him back toward our farm.

When they got here, my father built a bonfire. Some of the men wanted to tar and feather the sheriff, but they cheered instead when he threw some papers in the fire. Then he said that he thought it was only right that the farmers should own their land instead of paying rent and giving a share of their crops to Van Rensselaer. When he promised to try to make the landlord sell us our farms, he was finally sent packing. Then my mother invited the neighbors to stay for supper.

While supper was cooking, my father said, "Who blew the warning call?"

"Hannah did," my brother said. I blushed, but I felt very proud. My father's eyes twinkled and he picked me up and spun me around, pretending I was very heavy. "I declare, Hannah's gotten so big I think one of our calico shirts would fit her," he said, laughing. And a week later, after mother had made a few changes, I finally got my blue calico dress.